First published in the UK in 2008 by
QED Publishing
A Quarto Group company
226 City Road
London ECIV 2TT
www.qed-publishing.co.uk

A catalogue record for this book is available
from the British Library.

ISBN 978 1 84835 077 9

Author Kate Tym
Illustrator Sarah Wade
Editor Clare Weaver
Designer Alix Wood
Consultant David Hart

Publisher Steve Evans
Creative Director Zeta Davies

Printed and bound in China

Say PLEASE

QED MANNERS

KATE TYM

Illustrated by Sarah Wade

Peter and Ernie were **best friends.**

They did **everything** together.

At school, they sat on the same table.

Peter liked getting things done. When Mrs Tipping told them to make a dinosaur in junk-modelling time, Peter took charge.

Stick its head here, Ernie.

Ernie did as he was told.

And when Peter got his hand stuck to the table and Ernie helped him get unstuck with a bowl of warm water, did Peter say "Thank you"?

No, he said,

Oh, that's better. I'm starving. Come on, Ernie, let's get some lunch.

At the weekend, Ernie and Peter did things together, too.

You carry the fishing rods, Ernie.

Put the worm on the hook, Ernie.

Hold the net, Ernie.

Catch it, Ernie!

9

And when Peter sank into the mud and Ernie had to pull him out, did Peter say "Thank you"? No, he said,

Come on, Ernie, pack this stuff up. It's fish for supper tonight and I'm starving.

And even when it was Ernie's birthday party, Peter was just the same.

And when it was home time and Ernie made sure he gave Peter the party bag with the biggest piece of cake, did Peter say "Thank you"?

No, he said,

Can't wait to use your new football, Ernie. Now where's that piece of cake?

When the summer holidays came, Ernie's family went to stay at his aunt's house in the countryside for a whole two weeks.

"My aunt and my cousin are coming to stay in our house. You'll like my cousin Archie," Ernie said. "He's just like you!"

The next day, Ernie's cousin called round.

"Let's go into the garden," he said to Peter.
"You bring the football."

And when Archie kicked the ball into the neighbour's garden and sent Peter to fetch it, did he say "Please"?

16

No, he said, "All that
exercise has made
me hungry, have you
brought a packed lunch?"

17

Peter couldn't wait for Ernie to get home. Archie was bossy and rude and never asked nicely or said "Please". He *never* said "Thank you" either, even when Peter had *really* helped him out.

Peter got a funny feeling in his tummy. Had he treated Ernie the way Archie treated him?

Peter wrote Ernie a note.

Then Peter got to work. He decorated his room and made a big banner.

He baked a cake (with the help of his mummy)…

and made Ernie a present.

Welcome Home

Best Friend

When Ernie came round, he couldn't believe his eyes. Then, when Peter made his speech, he couldn't believe his ears.

"I'm ever so glad you're back!" said Peter. "Thank you for being my best friend."

"Didn't you like Archie, then?" asked Ernie.

"Not really," Peter admitted. "He was very bossy and rude."

"Oh," said Ernie. "You're right, Peter. Come to think of it, he is a bit like that. But do you know, you're nothing like him at all!"

Notes for parents and teachers

- Look at the front cover of the book together. Talk about the picture. Can the children guess what the book is going to be about? Read the title together.

- Explore with the children what it means to have a 'best friend'. Why is it nice to do lots of things with one person? Would that person know you really well? Would they know what you like or don't like?

- Peter and Ernie even sit together at school. Can the children think of any downsides of spending too much time with their best friend?

- Read pages 6 and 7 together. Ask the children what they think about how Peter is asking Ernie to do things. Is he asking him or telling him? Do they think the way Peter is speaking to Ernie is nice? If not, why not? What words do we use if we want to ask nicely?

- Look at Peter and Ernie's faces on page 9. Does one of them look happier than the other? Do the children think Peter has noticed that Ernie doesn't look very happy? Why might he not have noticed?

- Read page 11 with the children. Do they think Peter actually means to be helpful? If Peter asked in a different way, might Ernie feel he was being helpful? See if the children can re-phrase Peter's comments so that they sound polite and thoughtful. For example, "Would you like me to help you open that present, Ernie?"

- Ernie looks sad in the picture on page 12. Discuss with the children why that might be. Does the fact that it's his birthday make Peter's behaviour even more upsetting? What can we do on someone's birthday to make them feel special?

- On page 13, Ernie says Archie is just like Peter. What do the children think that means? What do they expect Archie to be like?

- Look at pages 14–19 together. Do the children think Archie is like Peter? How is he showing this? What does Peter look like now that someone's bossing him around?

- Why do the children think that Peter can't wait for Ernie to get home on page 20? Discuss why Peter gets a funny feeling in his tummy. How does he feel when he realizes that he didn't treat Ernie very nicely? Does he now realize what it's like to be in Ernie's shoes?

- Read and discuss pages 22–23. Why couldn't Ernie believe his eyes or his ears? How does it make him feel to have Peter do so much for him? Why does Ernie say that Peter is nothing like Archie? Do the children think he knows Peter is sorry?